Benedict Kiely was born in 1919 in Dromore, County Tyrone, the family moved to the town of Omagh a few years later. His father, a veteran of the Boer War, worked on the ordnance survey of Ulster. In 1937 Kiely entered a Jesuit seminary to study for the priesthood but after being hospitalised for a year suffering from spinal tuberculosis he left the seminary and studied for an Arts degree at University College Dublin.

Kiely settled in Dublin in 1944. After publishing his first book, *Counties of Contention* (a study of the partition of Ireland), he became a leader writer and columnist with the *Irish Independent*. His first novel, *Land without Stars*, was published in 1946, from 1951 to 1964 Kiely was the literary editor of the *Irish Press*. Alongside his work as a journalist Kiely also lectured at University College Dublin while publishing further novels and non-fiction, including his biography of the nineteenth-century novelist William Carleton, *Poor Scholar*.

In 1964 Kiely resigned from full-time journalism to teach creative writing at several American universities while also achieving popular fame in Ireland as a broadcaster, particularly on 'Sunday Miscellany'.

Benedict Kiely's enduring importance is, perhaps, due to his short stories, which are the equal of those of Sean O'Faolain and Frank O'Connor. He frequently published stories in *The New Yorker*. In his short stories Kiely drew on a tradition of rural storytelling as well as his deep love of Irish myth, music and folk culture. Benedict Kiely's writing is informed with a humanism and sense of history that is expressed in his most powerful novels, written as a response to the deepening sectarianism and violence of the Troubles in Northern Ireland, *Proxopera* (1977) and *Nothing Happens in Carmincross* (1985).

In 1981 Kiely was a founding member of Aosdána, an association of Ireland's major artists, and in 1996 he was elected Saoi of Aosdána, the highest honour an Irish writer can receive. His final major works were two volumes of autobiography, *Drink to the Bird* (1992) recalled his childhood in Omagh while *The Waves Behind Us* (1999) evoked Dublin's literary life with vivid descriptions of Brendan Behan and Patrick Kavanagh, among others.

Benedict Kiely died in 2007 but his work continues to be celebrated by the annual Benedict Kiely Literary Weekend, which is held in his native Omagh.

PROXOPERA

A Tale of Modern Ireland

PROXOPERA
A Tale of Modern Ireland

Benedict Kiely

TURNPIKE BOOKS

First published in Great Britain by Victor Gollancz, 1977
This edition published 2015 by Turnpike Books

turnpikebooks@gmail.com

ISBN 9780957233676

Printed and bound by Clays Ltd, St Ives plc

In Memory of
the Innocent Dead

Sea-lions and sharks, *alligators and whales with mouths that would swallow a truck* . . . .

That lake would never be the same again.

. . . *oh the sights that we saw as we waited for death on the treacherous waves of Lough Muck.*

Yet the birds, they say, sang around Dachau.

The waterfowl now swim on the still surface or fly around and cry around the circle of hills, harvest-coloured. The holidays are over and the dry rustle this year is early in the leaves. A dozen or more waterhens are in convention in a reedy corner near a sagging black boathouse. Only in one bay on the far shore is the silence disturbed by two black boats, moving slowly, men just barely using the oars or standing up and sitting down again. The sound of voices comes faintly across the water. He says to his son: the lake will never be the same again.

—The water never knew what was happening.

—I doubt that. Water may know more than we think. And grass. And old rocks. Think of all those old rocks that were around us in Donegal for the last three weeks. The lake looked as if it knew what was happening on the day of the water-skiing.

His son's wife who is a tall handsome red-headed girl with slightly prominent teeth, daring breasts and the faintest hint of an incipient double chin – very voluptuous, although he shouldn't be thinking along those lines – says that on the day of the water-skiing the lake was bright and dancing. On the night that thing happened the lake was dark and still. Wouldn't that make a difference?

He pats her on the shoulder affectionately as he climbs out from the back of the car where he has been sitting with the two children and a large glass jar containing two morose crabs rudely torn away from their homes on the Donegal shore.

She is an amusing imaginative girl.

—But no, he says, still waters run deep and all that. Water doesn't need light in order to see. Water is a sort of god. Or at any rate a goddess. That's what people thought long ago, they called rivers after goddesses.

The lake for sure had been a goddess on the day of the water-skiing. Never had he thought that he would see on his own lake the sort of thing you saw on the movies or television: Californian or Hawaiian beaches, galloping rollers, bouncing speed-boats, naked young women on surfboards, Arion on the dolphin's back, rising and falling, vanishing, reappearing through jewels of flying spray, spirits at one moment of the air and the water, marred by no speck of sordid earth. Was it better or worse to be young now than it was, say, forty-five years ago?

For him in his boyhood that lake had always been asleep. He lived in those days in the town three miles away. The walk from the town to the lake switchbacked over rolling farmland, root crops and oats, heavy black soil, solid square slated farmhouses, a well-planted Presbyterian countryside. After the first mile it was the custom for himself and his comrades to slither down an embankment where the road crossed the railway to the west and the ocean, to walk a hundred yards into a dank rock-cutting, to drink there from a spring that came on an iron spout out of the naked rock. That, for him, had been the well at the world's end mentioned in the old stories. No water had ever tasted like that water. One of the best meals he had ever eaten had been eaten there: raw turnips taken from a neighbouring field, cleaned at the spring and sliced, washed down by the clear ice-cold water. There was also the delight and danger of being caught there by a train, of crushing close to the dripping rock until the roaring belching monster passed.

Half a mile further on, the road went up a steep hill and into a tunnel of tall beeches. In the autumn and right on into January the leaves stayed so russet the road seemed warm. On the hilltop to the right hand and dominating the countryside stood a square, white, three-storeyed house inhabited then by an amazing family: strong, red-cheeked, flaxen-haired brothers and sisters, a dozen or more of them, he was never quite sure how many. They came, carrying bibles, to church in the town but never all of them at the same time. The popular report was that under that roof brothers and sisters knew each other as brothers and sisters conventionally shouldn't: it was a fascinating idea.

From the top of the hill you had a choice of routes: to the right the longer one, uphill, down dale, passing a place where there was a wooden bridge over the bend of a river, going round the world for sport, by fifty farms, a corrugated-iron-roofed Orange hall where there had been a bloody row one night because some guileless, love-deludhered young Orangeman had brought a Catholic girl to a dance, and by half-a-hundred ridges and bridges to rejoin the shorter route at a crossroads and go on the level to the lakeshore.

The shorter road ran straight along a spine of sandy, heathery, esker land where once the glaciers had stopped. Below, in a hollow of quaking bog was a small lake, surrounded by sallies and bog-birch, in which demented old ladies and others were continually drowning themselves. There was an almost vocal sadness about the place. Association? Or had it been melancholy to begin with: right from the beginning of time, from the melting of the glaciers? That little lake as far as he knew had never had a name.

From the crossroads where the two routes rejoined, the road went again under splendid beech trees, the lake, a white light, widening and brightening at the end of a tunnel until it burst on you in all its delight, only a few miles all round but an almost perfect oval, a black boathouse to the right and boats dancing attendance in a semi-circle in front of it, a half-mile around the gravelly lakeshore road the bright red timber of the jetty and diving-boards at the swimming-club.

These dark days the swimming-club didn't function any more. The water-skiing had been a heroic attempt to give that sort of life back to the lake. The last attempt? The lake would never be the same again.

The murmur of voices still comes across the water from the men searching and searching in a bay among the reeds, in a bay that had been the best place of all for perch on those long-lost sunny days.

July was the best month for perch and the best day was the twelfth. It was folklore that the Orangemen always got a sunny day for their procession of bands and banners in honour of King William of Orange and the Battle of the Boyne. Up to the age of twelve or so the band and the banners were what the Americans called fun things: fifes and pipes and brass and melodeons, kettle drums, big drums, and giant drums beaten – merely to make a rolling rhythmical bedlam that might bring down rain on the Sahara – with bamboo canes by sweating coatless men with bleeding knuckles. Often it took two men to carry one of those drums, one fore, the actual drummer (naturally) aft. The best drummer was the man who smashed the most canes, even the most hides. Odd as the jungle it all was, bongo, bongo, bongo, I don't want to leave the Congo! but what the hell? The marching men wore coloured sashes. On the silken picture-banners King William on a white horse went splashing across the Boyne, or Queen Victoria sat on a throne and handed a bible to a kneeling negress and the legend said: The secret of England's greatness.

Then after twelve or so you began to think and the thing wasn't funny any more, wasn't just parade and pantomime, and the giant drums were actually saying something. Like: To hell with the Pope, Croppies Lie Down, We'll kick Ten Thousand Papishes right over Dolly's Brae, Slewter, slaughter, holy water, harry the Papishes every one, drive them under and cut them asunder the Protestant boys will carry the drum.

What it was all about was hate which, as always, bred hate, and suddenly you were sick of the town on that day and the lake was paradise.

Like the Orangemen the perch shoaled and were lively in the heat and the sunshine – and hungry for bait. Heat haze clouded the sun. Ripening oats on hills around the lake stood motionless as sheets of bronze. From green hills cattle stampeded to the shore to wade in until the water lipped their bellies, to stand lashing hopelessly with their tails against relentless clegs. The surface of the lake was dark and quiet except that once in a while an arc of little ripples would move on it, coming from nowhere, vanishing suddenly, and a breeze like a quick kiss from a ghost would touch a sweaty forehead and be gone again, and after that the perch would move, mad as mackerel, tearing the water as if the low hot skies were raining rocks, and all you had to do was pull them in, big and little, striped black and green and orange, fine fighters, big dorsal fins opening and closing, in outrage and despair, like Japanese fans.

The best corners in the lake were in there beyond the boat-house where the reeds were so high you were almost but not quite cut off from the rest of the world: or over there where men in black boats were still probing and dredging Almost but not quite. For through a gap in the reeds you could, as you waited for the perch, look across the waters at the white house. Reeds made one frame for the picture. Beech trees set back from the avenue that led up to the house made another. There were other houses, Orange and Green or Protestant and Catholic, on the hills around the lakeshore, but they were simple thatched cottages and nothing at all in the bay-windowed, wide-fronted style of the white house. He had always envied the people who owned it, the lawn and flower-beds before it, the barns and varied outbuildings behind it. He had missed strikes and earned mockery from his companions by sitting heedlessly, absorbed in envy of the people who lived in that house, long and white, an air of aristocratic age about it: and, the most beautiful thing of all, cutting across a corner of the lawn a small brook tumbling down to join the lake. To have your own stream on the lawn was the height of everything.

In reveries now between sleeping and waking, relaxed in a deck chair on a sunny lawn and looking at the lake through half-closed eyes, he liked to tell himself that he had always known he would own and live in that house. That wasn't so. He may have wished that he one day would, but however could he have known. Premonitions were notions you had after the event.

Here they all were now, his son and son's wife and their two children, all happy after their Donegal holiday, the children tired but still talkative, the displaced crabs motionless as the rocks they came from: and himself. All being driven slowly by his daughter-in-law between deep banks and hedges into the farmyard, home again, and out of the car now, the children suddenly energetic again and racing in circles around the yard like hounds released from kennels, running to this and that corner to see if everything is as they had left it.

Behind the hayshed the three great sycamores are dark and motionless in the evening. Not one of the party seems as yet to have a premonition about anything. Well, perhaps the sycamores, perhaps the crabs.

All the way back from Dungloe in Donegal the streams they crossed had been in a brown foaming fresh. The rains and tempest of last week, the Lammas floods coming early this year, and now sunshine that by the texture of it would last until Christmas. Countless bees are still hard at it in the pink-oxalis borders that his son's wife loves so well because of the radiance that opens to the sun, because she has her flourishing apiary in the orchard beyond the hayshed. And the benefit of heather-blossom into the bargain from a small patch of turbary within beesflight and on the lakeshore.

The bees in the pink blossoms, the breeze in the sycamores make the only sound. There is suddenly something too much about the silence.

The pink borders, living with bees, go all round the yard, backed by the white barns and byres and stables, doors and windows outlined in red. Nothing moves but the bees. He stands alone, ten paces from the car, and breathes in the peace and is inexplicably perturbed.

The little boy runs towards the hayshed where three weeks ago there was a litter of cocker pups. The little girl dances towards the back porch of the house. She calls: Minnie, Minnie Brown, we're home again from Dungloe town.

On the journey home he has composed that rhyme for her. Minnie is the housekeeper and it is odd in a way that she hasn't been out in the yard to meet them.

His broadbacked son walks towards the red half-door of one of the stables. The harriers ride no more in these times but he still keeps and pastures two amiable hacks. A stout quick-tempered man who too early, and much to his own chagrin, has gone completely bald and whose jacket never buttons without obvious strain. The back of his egg-shaped head is comic.

His wife, a full-bodied red wine, goes gracefully after her little daughter.

He stands where he is, simply looking at his house, at his people, at the sycamores, at the last fifty years. Time stands still. The little boy comes running back from the hayshed. Trotting rather. His head down and sideways as if he were playing ponies. He pulls, pulling a bellrope, at his granda's jacket. He says: Granda, there's a funny man in the hayshed.

Granda already knows. The man has stepped out into the open. He has a shotgun. He wears a felt-brimmed hat and a gasmask. The mask has been slashed at the mouth for the sake of sound but the effect still is as if somebody with laryngitis were trying to talk through tissue paper and a comb. He says: Freeze. Everybody freeze.

As in the best or the worst gangster films except that the hoodlums talk and act cool and this fellow seems to be nervous: All of you freeze. Granda says: Including the children?

He picks the boy up in his arms. The man advances, pointing the shotgun. The wheezes say, almost as if the creator of the wheezes had a cleft palate: One false step. Into the house. All of you. We're all inside.

They walk towards the house. He comes behind them. Not all inside the house. Because another masked man steps out from the laurels and rhododendrons to the right. He has a sock or something over his face. Carries a pistol. Wears a workman's tin hat.

His son walks before him, the back of his neck now red with anger. Even his egghead seems to be changing colour. He says: Who are you? What the hell is this?

—We'll let you know a chara, the second man says.

He has a sharp clear voice and something like a Cork accent: Inside, everybody inside.

This is the first time that I have ever been ordered into my own house. He is for a moment paralysed with anger. He watches his daughter-in-law carrying her daughter and bending under the lintel, the doorway is low, then his son, the back of his neck on fire with fury and the mark of Donegal sunburn, then Gasmask waving the shotgun. The ass of Gasmask's trousers is shiny and hangs low. There's something familiar-looking about his feet. Holding the little boy whose heart beats like the heart of a captive bird he stands stiffly on his own threshold.

—Keep it moving, old man.

That's Corkman speaking.

—Why should I? What hell right has a lout like you to order me about in my own house?

—This right.

It is, of course, the gun poking into the small of his back. This is cowboy country.

—I'm hardly worth shooting. Or kneecapping. The knees anyway aren't working as well as they used to.

—You're an old fellow, we know. But don't make things hard for anybody else. Children can be kneecapped.

—You would too. All for Ireland. Or is it Orange Ulster? But then you're from Cork.

—Less talk. Inside. Deliver the goods. That's all you have to do.

With a child in his arms and a pistol at his back he hasn't much choice. From the kitchen, as he walks a tiled corridor and across the wide scullery, he hears the sound of the television: whizzes, bangs, the clanking of machinery. So that the coloured screen is, ludicrously, the first thing to catch his eye. Against a blue sky a fighter-plane is falling, twisting, leaving behind it a spiral of black smoke. The Battle of Britain. Then he sees Minnie, stiff as a stick in a high wooden armchair. Gagged and bound. In a rough Belfast accent the third man says: Wizard prangs. And the bastards of Brits wouldn't even give us the credit for Paddy Finnucane. They say no Irishman was killed in the Battle of Britain.

Corkman says: Fuck you and Paddy Finnucane. Turn that bloody thing off. What do you think you're on? Your holidays?

Gasmask twists the knob. The plane hasn't yet touched earth. What is it about Gasmask's feet?

—Uncork the old dame. She can't do any damage now.

The third man, wearing a black felt mask that covers all his face, and an old-style British soldier's peaked cap, steps forward from the window bay: with no gun showing but with a hunting-knife at his belt. He unsheathes the knife, hacks away the gag, and the ropes that bind Minnie to the chair. They lie where they fall. Minnie moves her arms stiffly. Given time her tongue will get going. Not even the odd terrifying feeling of talking to a mask will keep Minnie mute.

—You're welcome home all of you and God bless you, she says, even if it wasn't much of a reception you got.

She slobbers a little. Her jaws and tongue are still stiff from the gag. She is a tall, brown-faced, wrinkled witch of a woman who always dresses in black for the husband who deserted her when they were three years married and that was forty years ago. The story as she tells it at Christmastime, or on the few other occasions when her memory is unfrozen by festivity, always follows the same formula: We tracked him everywhere, even as far as Newcastle-on-Tyne where he vanished without trace. We heard he joined the British army under a false name. But I know to God that even if he called himself Montgomery he wouldn't be taken in the Coldcream Gurkhas.

She stands up stiffly. She says: You'll want some refreshment after the long journey. At any rate you had a happy holiday. I got all the postcards you sent me. And Catherine, how are you? and Gary boy, don't be frightened. It's just that I wasn't that well able to greet ye when ye came in. But I'll make it up to ye when these blackguards are gone.

The children go to her silently and stand holding on to the long black skirt that recalls treachery and desertion and a man too worthless to be taken in an imaginary regiment, named contemptuously.

—Sit down old lady, Corkman says. Keep the children with you if you like.

—Thank you for nothing, Paddy from Cork. And who are you to tell me to sit down in my own kitchen?

—Sit down, for Christ's sake, and don't try my patience. You can cook everything in the house in half an hour. First, I've something to say.

—If you speak as well as you look you should be worth listening to.

—If you don't sit down we'll knock you on the head and tie you up again.

The voice behind the sock has risen an octave. She says: You're a hero. A grown man with a gun in his fist isn't afraid of any old woman.

But she is herself afraid and the children sense it. They cling to her. Catherine begins to sob.

—Oh Jesus, says Gasmask, I hate to hear children cry.

Corkman says: You should be running a creche. Suffer the little children. Sit down, you old hag, while your kneecaps still allow you to bend your knees.

—Wait a minute, his son says.

And takes a step forward. But Corkman tilts the pistol upwards and there is a silence broken only by the little girl's sobs, and that seems to last for a long time until Corkman laughs, a rich, hearty, surprisingly good-natured laugh. He says: There's many a fat farmer whose heart would break in two if he could see the townland that we are riding to. Dear gracious old lady would you for the last time, and for the love and honour of Almighty God, sit down and shut up and keep the children quiet?

She's frightened, more by the masks he'd say than by any horrors that she, at her age and coming out of another time, can readily imagine. Even though she reads the papers every day and clucks her tongue and says Sacred Heart of Jesus over outrage after outrage she has not yet fully realised the nature of the deeds now being done – for Ireland or what they call Ulster. Masks and queer faces and painted devils she can understand and she knows that they are evil: Lucifer looked like that once upon a time with the addition of horns and tail and a cow's foot. Yet, frightened or not, she does not give up easily: I'll sit down when Mr Binchey asks me to sit down. Either of them. They are the masters in this house. And gentlemen into the bargain.

Under the sock Corkman hisses like a serpent. Binchey senior realises with guilt that he has been enjoying or at least studying this struggle of wills between an old woman and a madman in a mask. Binchey junior, isolated and furious and helpless where the pistol has halted him in the middle of the floor, says hoarsely and so unexpectedly that it sounds like a startled shout: Sit down, Minnie. We'll hear what the man has to say.

The hissing ceases. It has been a most deliberate performance. Corkman says: Well said, Mr Binchey Two. *Ex ore infantium* or out of the mouths of babes and sucklings. Thanks for consenting to listen. I don't want to be forced to show you who for the moment is master in this house. But I want you two men to listen carefully. If everybody plays ball nobody will get hurt.

The children, silent again, are together between Minnie's long legs, faces to her midriff like frightened sheep at a fair.

—If the three of you would sit together on that couch for the sake of concentration like, we could get down to business. What time is it now?

Gasmask tells him. He pulls a chair close to the couch and sits looking at an angle at father and son and the woman between them. He says: We'll have a wait but it can't be helped. The stuff isn't here yet. We can't move until light, tomorrow morning, when the good people are going to Sunday mass.

—What in hell do you mean? You're telling us nothing.

That was Binchey Two.

—Patience brother. I'll explain. I want Binchey One here to do a little milk delivery. To one of two spots in the town. He'll even have a choice. This is a free democratic society.

—My father-in-law, she says, can't drive any more.

Binchey Two says: I'll do it.

Corkman is hissing again, steam escaping. What sort of a mind is in there behind the sock?

—Jesus, give us credit for some savvy. We know you're suspended for dangerous and drunken driving. The first Royal Ulster cunt of a constable that saw you would pull you in. The town wouldn't get its milk delivery.

—It's a proxy bomb.

—How bright you are, fat farmer.

—Afraid to do your own dirty work.

—Stuff it. Too many pigs spoil the breath. They say that when you were in college you used to go to the cattle-market in the morning to get dung on your boots to let the world know you were doing agriculture.

Soldier's Cap, who sits straddle on a chair, his back to the low bay-window, the light fading through the blood-red leaves of Virginia creeper, and who is honing his hunting knife on the heel of his hand, laughs hoarsely, Gasmask stands by the door, butt of his shotgun grounded, at attention almost, a soldier of the Republic. What the hell is it about his feet? Gasmask says nothing. Binchey Two is very red in the face and in the bald head: The smell was better in the cattle-market, and that goes for you. Put down the gun and step outside and we'll see how much pigshit you contain.

—Easy, easy, fat man. We're here on business.

—Keep it that way.

Minnie whoops and cackles: It was a fair gentleman's challenge.

The hissing must make the sock uncomfortably damp. Gasmask shifts his feet and gun-butt: behind the mask he could be alarmed. The woman says: Take it easy, everybody. My father-in-law has been forbidden to drive. He has a heart condition.

—The police don't know that.

—He could drop at the wheel.

—He can drive carefully. Lady, we all have heart conditions.

Binchey senior says that nowadays a man is lucky to have any sort of a condition, or a heart to tick or a knee to bend: What do you want me to drive and where?

—You'll do it.

—I don't have much choice.

—You're a reasonable man.

—I wouldn't count on it.

The woman says: The people will wonder if they see him driving.

—They will like fuck, Soldier's Cap says. They'll just think he's so mean he can't keep his hands off the wheel.

Again the coarse laugh. He has a gravelly recognisable voice. With the exception of Corkman these are local people, for Gasmask's feet are as familiar as fireirons. Soldier's Cap knows that he still has an interest in the hackney-car business that his father, who was also a saddler, founded. Corkman walks slowly, blowing into his pistol, to where Soldier's Cap sits straddle in the bay of the window. They wait uneasily for blows and discipline. The children have not moved. Minnie murmurs to them and strokes their heads. Corkman stoops and whispers, hissing, and Soldier's Cap leaps up as if he had been electrocuted, sheathes the hunting-knife, stands rigid as a guardsman. The last light is dying behind the red creepers. Binchey Two sullenly repeats to Corkman: I can easily do the driving. Who'll stop me on a Sunday morning?

—Your license is suspended.

—Like you don't want to do anything illegal. My father has bad sight as well as a weak heart.

—He can drive slow and wear his glasses. Look, farmer boy, we've been over this.

The woman says: I drove back from Donegal.

—Lady, we can't send a woman out with the goods.

—Chivalry, says Binchey One.

—Dear Christ, Corkman hisses, we have enough to do fighting the Brits, without listening to your bullshit.

—Fight the Brits, says Binchey Two, to the last Catholic shop in the village of Belleek or the town of Strabane. Man, you love the Brits, you couldn't exist without them. The nickname is affectionate. They give you the chance to be Irish heroes. They give you targets you can easily see.

In a low strained voice, controlling hysteria, the woman says: Stop it, all of you. Let's get this over with. There are the children.

—Sense, lady, says Corkman. I could do biz with you.

Before her man can again explode, she says: The occasion won't arise. But tell us, for God's sake, what the drill is.

—Simple. Sometime during the night a creamery can will be delivered here. All you have to do is drive it into the town and leave it in one of two places.

—What happens to the car?

—You're well insured, farmer boy.

Soldier's Cap says: Commandeered by the freedom fighters.

But the silence that Corkman allows to settle for a while after that remark indicates to Soldier's Cap that his words are unwanted.

—Suppose, says Binchey One, that we all refuse to do it.

—You won't. There are children. And the women. We don't want to be rough.

There's an even longer silence and then Minnie's voice, low and hoarse: Harm a hair on their heads and I'll pray prayers on you and yours.

—Jesus, Gasmask says.

But Corkman tells the old woman to be quiet: Pray not for me nor on me but for yourselves and for your children.

—You mock God's words, Minnie says.

—Jesus, Gasmask says, I don't like this.

He shuffles uneasily from one familiar foot to another.

—It'll be a nice quiet time, says Corkman. But plenty people on the roads going to mass and meeting. The Brits and the R.U. cunts will be keeping a low profile. Put the children to bed, old woman. You (he means Soldier's Cap) go with her and keep your big mouth shut. One place is the entryway between the town hall and the post office. But if the security there is too tight the next best place is the avenue between Judge Flynn's house and the golf-club. Very close to the Judge. We have the women and the children and your fine fat son. Remember that.

—I'll remember. I'll remember it for a long time.

—No threats, old man. You're in no fucking position.

—Judge Flynn is one of the best men in the north.

—The more reason he shouldn't be where he is. He lends credit to the system.

Soldier's Cap, who has returned, ventures to say that Judge Flynn is a tool of imperialism. No comment from Corkman.

—So you kill a man more readily because he's a good man. And blow up the town hall and post office. What's the point?

—You could call it a reprisal, Corkman says, for what they found in the lake.

And the lake would never be the same again.

The undulating movement of the skiers, the sweeping curves made by the speed-boats, the wash and the perturbation of the waters could have brought the body up from the depths. Over there in that corner where, now that twilight has fallen, the men in the black boats have suspended their search for the murder weapon.

The body was badly decomposed. Forensic scientists said that it had been in the water for some time. You'd hardly need to be a forensic scientist to guess that much. Never knew before that we had a forensic scientist in the town or district. They could, though, have brought them from Belfast. Or the army may bring a truckload of them with it wherever it goes. Badly needed nowadays.

But with or without them it was a fair guess that the body might have been in the lake from the night of the evening on which the man who owned it didn't come home from work. Lying weighted down there in the dark until the movement of life on the day of the water-skiing drew it up from the mud at the roots of the reeds.

That water-skiing would be the lake's last effort to laugh. *Sea-lions and sharks, alligators and whales*. A man I know wrote a good comic song about that lake and that line was part of the chorus.

An early-morning fisherman, idling in one of those black boats, saw the floating body in that quiet corner among the reeds. A wire that had come unwound led to a fifty-six pound weight sunk deep in the mud. The man had been in his thirties and was the father of four children. Last seen alive when he locked his public-house in the town to drive his white Mazda car the three miles to his rural home. When he didn't get home at his usual time his wife raised the alarm. Bloodstains and shirt-buttons were discovered in the laneway leading to his house. A neighbour said he had heard five shots fired in the dusk.

For two weeks after, hundreds of people walked with the police and their tracker dogs scouring the country. Nobody seemed to suspect the lake because it was far away in another direction. So the water-skiing went happily ahead. But murderers in the dark had made the sleeping lake their accomplice. The innocent lake had been forced to share the guilt. The lake, out there and fading into another dusk, the lake knew. It could never be the same again.

Corkman is speaking: They killed him because some of us used his pub.

He wasn't one of us. But he was with us. We'll get them.

—They say ye shot him because he spoke against murder gangs at a town council meeting.

—Mind your manners, old man.

—Manners, says Binchey Two.

—Anyway, it's a fucking lie. We'll get them.

—You'll get who, Binchey One asks. The town hall. The post office? Judge Flynn who sure as God had nothing to do with it?

—We'll show them we're active. That we can plant bombs where we like.

—Big deal. When my father does it for you.

—Stuff it, farmer.

His hand, a long bony pale hand, has tightened on the pistol. It could also be a damp hand.

The women and children have been locked into Minnie's basement bedroom. They have been told that their men's lives depend on their conduct. But as an extra precaution Soldier's Cap has been ordered outside to watch the bedroom window, to watch the world around them. He clearly doesn't like the detail but he goes. The dishonoured lake lies uneasily in the darkness: *Oh the sights that we saw as we waited for death on the treacherous waves of Lough Muck.*

Binchey One says: Judge Flynn stands for justice and peace.

—Old man, for an old man who was a famous teacher you've no head on your shoulders. They'll blame the people who put the body in the lake. Who wants peace?

—Logic, says Binchey Two. We. They. Them. Us. Who, in Christ's name, is who? Everybody wants peace except the madmen.

—Big words, farmer boy. We're not dealing with logicians. Let me tell you a story.

Seated on a chair by the door that leads to the night outside, and the lake and the town, Gasmask crosses his legs and, dear God, I know now what's familiar about his feet, his father's feet, poor civil shambling sod. In the corner on the floor behind him there's a child's tricycle, red with green wheels, and a doll's pram, the doll sitting upright and staring, lonely for three weeks while her playmate was in Donegal, still lonely, and surprised that no hugs and kisses have come her way for the homecoming.

—The little girl, he says, may need her doll.

—See to it, Corkman says.

And Gasmask stands up on his father's awkward feet and, with his shotgun trailing, wheels the pram out the other door and along the corridor to Minnie's room. The severed ropes and gag still lie where they fell. What has happened to the two crabs in the jar? The dead have peace but they don't know it.

—Let me tell both of you a story to show you the sort of animals we're dealing with.

Binchey Two says: Public relations.

Corkman ignores him. He tells his story.

—There were three U.V.F. men came over from the murder triangle by Portadown to kill a Catholic in Newtownstewart. Two hit men and one man to finger the subject. When they got there the man's away in Dublin. They go into a pub in Newtownstewart and start to drink. Then the fingerman says he knows another papish who would be better dead. They set out to get him. But he has emigrated to Canada. Feeling very bad they go back to the pub in Newtownstewart. On the way home, well drunk, they stop in Gortin Gap for a piss and the gunmen shoot the fingerman because he couldn't find anybody for them to shoot. One of their own. Think of that, old man.

—Quite right they were, says Binchey Two. He wasted a whole day on them. Time's money in your business.

—You'll push me too far, farmer boy.

—Go out and tar and feather a few girls. To keep your hand in.

—Jesus, I'll kneecap you just for the fun of it.

—Kneecaps are up in the Tam Ratings, the popularity polls. You don't know who you are until you look at your knees. I made you a fair offer. Put down the gun and step outside.

—Jesus.

Corkman is on his feet, the pistol coming up. Binchey One steps in front of him.

—Enough. Both of you. One shot and I'm through.

And to his son: Keep it cool. This will all be over by noon. Think of the women.

Corkman says: You should have whipped sense into him before he went bald. Men have been shot for less.

They are all seated again except Gasmask who stands shifting from one awkward foot to the other, his back to the wide window. Corkman orders him to pull the curtains. And to Binchey One: Get what rest you can. I want you fresh for the morning.

The curtains are drawn. Gasmask hisses: The shades of night are falling fast.

—A poet, says Binchey Two, by God a poet.

—As regards the men in Gortin Gap, Binchey One says, it makes more sense than to murder Judge Flynn because he's a good man. More of you should kill each other. Go to the

Greenland Cap and settle whatever it is between ye and leave normal people alone.

Bearing the bomb, an angel of death, he will in the morning drive past the graveyard in which his wife is buried. *Soles occidere possunt et redire.* The back of the couch is hard against his spine. This is a rare way to keep a vigil. St. Ignatius, turning his back on the sword and vowing himself to Christ and to Christ his mother, had, in the mad manner of the man from La Mancha, watched all night over his armour. *Nobis cum semel occidit brevis lux.* There would be no time to stop to say a prayer at the graveside. The urgent business of Ireland did not nowadays allow time for prayer. *Nox est perpetua, una dormienda. Da mihi basia mille.*

No time to walk crunching up the gravel path, past the graves of men and women who were still alive in his memory. The tall tweedy jeweller, a great man to fish trout and salmon, prematurely bald like my pugnacious son, who had married such a handsome brunette, much younger than himself, from another town, that he was the envy of every man. Mysteriously, she died young and the tall lean man fished no more, spoke little and only to few and, among his jewels and trinkets and chimney clocks, withered away.

The two main paths in the graveyard are cruciform, Protestants to the left as you enter, Catholics to the right, the cross that had divided them in life divided them also in death: on one arm of the cross the grave of my father and mother and beside it my wife, a controversial placing perhaps, since she had been born and died a Protestant, and beside her the grave of that big happy companion of my youth, six years older than me, with whom I used to go shooting and fishing. He taught me the ways of guns and the ways of women, and became a military doctor and, in some dark night in the early days of the Hitler war, shot himself in his rooms in Aldershot camp in Britain. *Soles occidere possunt et redire.* Catullus also was a great friend to me in those days, when I, as people used to say, wooed her and won her, one day in the High Street her father halting me, at the beginning of my summer holidays in my second year in college, and asking me would I grind his daughter in Latin for her senior certificate.

That lovely old thatched farmhouse, pointed eaves, and dormer windows cowled in the thatch, apple-orchards all around it, at a crossroads a mile north-east of the town: can't remember who lives in it now. Happy hours, heads together over Allen's Latin grammar or Ritchie's Latin composition, and Livy and Tacitus and Virgil and Horace, and Catullus, my favourite, who naturally was not on any secondary-school course but, *da mihi basia mille.* I could even quote a lot of Catullus in those days and I had a good voice. The evening the hem of her school uniform skirt caught on her case of books as she lifted it from the floor to the table, and the skirt came up with the case and my breath caught a bit as I saw for the first time the perfections of that body, her burning innocence. Standing behind her where she sat and quoting Catullus and looking down on the white northern slopes of her breasts and thinking of the warm south, the true, the blushful Hippocrene: and one breast in time was to be cut away for cancer leaving behind it a strange, chaste champain about which she used to make jokes, almost lewd for her. But even that sacrifice could not halt the cancer.

The evening I asked her father could I marry her, and he said yes, he walked with me to the edge of the town where the roads meet and he talked with melancholy about what was to come on Europe and the world. A tall handsome man with a Roman profile and dark hair, not a rib of grey in it, parted up the middle. He was a tea and whiskey salesman, and ineluctable war would ruin his livelihood. He said: We lived through one big war. We won't be able to stand a second. The world will never be the same again.

He was dead in six months. Coronary? Melancholy? He lies buried with his wife and a son who died of wounds after Dunkirk. On the other arm of the cross. There will be no time, either, to pray at his grave.

Corkman sits, his elbows on the kitchen table, the pistol on the board before him. He is silent but very much awake. His son, with his head in his hands, seems asleep – but restlessly. Gasmask is snoring in Minnie's rocking-chair. Through the slit in the mask the snores make a sound that was never heard before. For sure and certain these distorted faces are out of a nightmare. Soldier's Cap is making out as well as he may in the shrubbery, with the cold promise that the watch will be changed at three in the morning. Corkman's tin hat has tilted and the sock-orsomething, misshapen over his face, makes him like a Guy Fawkes or that Colonel Lundy the Orangemen used to burn annually in effigy in happy memory of the siege of Derry. *From Antrim crossing over in sixteen eighty-eight, a plumed and belted lover came to the Ferry Gate.* That was the Earl of Tyrconnel. *She summoned to defend her, our sires, a beardless race. With shouts of No Surrender, they slammed it in his face.*

The Apprentice Boys of Protestant Derry, the Maiden City, close the gate before Tyrconnel and the troops of James Stuart. The long memory lives on. With riots and ructions and bombs and bloody Sundays as much a maiden now as Dresden on the morning after.

All this he says to Corkman. No comment. Gasmask creaks and rocks in the chair. The snores ride on like advancing shingly waves.

—The Cambridge rapist, he says, had a better mask than any of you. More imagination. You must have seen a picture of it in the papers. Like a great black pointy bonnet with a long zipper where the mouth should be. He had sewn hair all around the bottom of it so that it looked as if he had long hair and a beard.

No comment from Corkman.

—And white eyebrows painted above the eye-holes. And painted in white on the forehead or what covered it the simple word: Rapist. He wasn't, do you see, ashamed of his craft, trade or profession. When a girl woke up and looked up and read that in the middle of the night she knew right away what was in store for her.

No comment.

—What could you write on your forehead?

From behind his cupped clutched hands Binchey Two says: Cain. No comment.

—The chief constable in Cambridge blamed the case on the prevalence of unchecked porn. A dangerous word to use. It could have been misprinted.

—Old man, you talk too much.

—It's an old man's privilege.

—You don't have any privileges until you deliver the goods.

—After that, says Binchey Two, you could send him a 1916 medal.

No comment.

Binchey One says that according to Irenaeus in Edmund Spenser's Viewe of the State of Ireland the kerns and gallowglasses oppressed all men, spoiled their own people as well as the enemy, stole, were cruel and bloody and full of revenge, delighted in deadly execution, were licentious, swearers and blasphemers, common ravishers of women and murderers of children.

—He didn't like the Irish, old man. We know you taught Latin and history and English literature. It had to be English. We know what your history was like.

—You know a lot for a stranger to these parts.

—I do my homework.

Gasmask's snores trample onwards towards a gravelly coast.

He is wandering through London streets with his wife. They are planning a trip by water to the country but they fall asleep in a pub or in a flat and can't get to the boat. We meet a young official who asks me to telephone Mary Cluskey that in my youth I rolled in the ditches with, on the expert advice of that big happy man who died in Aldershot by his own hand. And when I'm talking to Mary on the 'phone I can still hear my wife's voice in the background. I keep asking Mary to pass the 'phone on to her but when she tries to, my wife is gone. Then she reappears, walking along Kensington High Street and carrying two travelling bags. She says she won't go to wherever it was we were going because I would only torment myself and her. Kensington High Street becomes a clay road between shambles of outhouses. We meet a crowd of boys playing with dogs and ask them the way to Hampstead. We have been going the wrong way, and an adult, a dwarf, Dickens' Daniel Quilp, redirects us. We sit down to eat at a rough wooden table and in the open air. My son is there as a boy, and his sister, grown-up, the image of her mother. In a dry, deep-sunken dyke to my left are bundles of antique books, weather-stained, mouldering. Then a girl at a little table, also to my left, produces tickets for a raffle and I am sharing a room with an Old Christian Brother who taught me in secondary school and had slight homosexual tendencies. There are two beds in the room, hospital screens, the floor slopes steeply down from one wall to the other, my bed is behind a screen in the corner farthest from the door. The old brother's pupils are doing exams and doing badly and in the dusk there is the slapping of buttock-flogging (he was an adept) and wailing from an adjacent building. In his bed I fall asleep but, perhaps wisely, go to my own bed when he comes in, and Mary Cluskey is there. Then the room is full of autumn leaves blown in through a window and the door, which is swinging open in the wind. Mary is picking up the leaves. She is pleasantly naked. The door slams shut.

And Gasmask has snored and rocked himself out of the chair and is picking himself up from the floor. The whole room is awake. Corkman says: Go out, for God's sake, and relieve Charlie Chaplin. Keep awake. Don't frighten the birds.

He has for a long time had recurrent nightmares about books left to rot and decay in the open air, sometimes in heaps or bound bundles, sometimes, even more crazily, on orderly shelves. He was also at the deathbed of that old Christian Brother in Baldoyle in Dublin. The old man had had a happy and holy death. On the Chinese mission he had picked up the passion for boys and buttock-whipping. He had had two brothers in the flesh who committed suicide and to the end, almost, he had a fear that he would go that way.

His son, yawning, stretching himself, says out of nowhere: It was simply that I preferred the cattle-market, to the college. There was more brains there. And, believe it or not, less shit.

No comment from Corkman.

Then knocks and footsteps round the house, whistles after dark. Corkman gives his pistol to Soldier's Cap: Watch this pair. Your life's on it. That's the milk delivery.

There has been no sound of a car engine. That could mean that the milk delivery has been prepared in and carried from somewhere close by. Or did the car stop a distance away so as not to draw attention to the house? It would be odd to think that somebody in a neighbouring cottage could all the time have been plotting and preparing this. His son says: One day when I was in primary school I was walking home through Fountain Lane where the soldiers' girls lived. Two of them were having an argy-bargy and one of them called the other a hoor. So being all of eight years of age I went right home and asked my mother what was a hoor? She laughed until she cried. She said: You'll find out soon enough. There's a fair share of them in this town.

—Next morning I'm on my way back through Fountain Lane and one of the pair is leaning out over the half-door, red in the face, hair in the eyes. She shouted at me: Wee fella, did you pass many worms this morning?

—That puzzled me for a long time. You see I couldn't recall seeing or overtaking any worms.

Something's going on outside. The gentlemen go by. Five and twenty ponies trotting through the dark, brandy for the parson, baccy for the clerk, laces for a lady, letters for a spy, watch the wall my darling . . .

—That's life for you, his son says. Or a lot of it. Hoors and worms. Worms and hoors.

No comment from Soldier's Cap. Corkman has come back. He says: That was the milk delivery, the creamery can. Brace yourself old man. You might yet be the first of your breed to die for Ireland.

Standing with one foot in the stone-flagged corridor and one in the basement bathroom, holding his shotgun as if he were behind a covered wagon and waiting for Indians, Gasmask hisses: Be careful Mr. Binchey. And good luck.

Binchey One is in shirt and trousers, and washing and shaving. This is a job he needs to be fresh for: Oh weep, my own town, for after all these years of love I carry death to your threshold.

Carefully he combs back his plentiful silver hair. It changed colour after she died but it stayed with me. When he was younger and drank more than was good for him he always had a fancy that if your hair was combed you looked sober. He soaks a face-cloth in cold water and swabs his face, particular attention to the ears so that I'll hear the bomb if it goes off prematurely. Do you hear the bomb that kills you? On the western front the old sweats said that you didn't hear the whistle of the shell that had your name on it. Yet how could anybody know if nobody lived to tell the tale? He says: That's the oddest bloody wish I ever heard, Bertie.

He hadn't meant to use the name but the harm's done now, if it is harm. Gasmask doesn't move. Or Bertie. He may be seeing Indians. He hisses: Search me. Silence is golden.

With those temporary speech-defects he should eschew sibilants.

—Your father's feet, Bertie.

—I'm saying nothing.

—I'd know them anywhere.

—For God's sake don't let him know you know me.

—Are you afraid of him?

—He's hell on wheels. He might hear us.

—He can't with the sound of the rashers frying.

And also the voices of children who seem blessedly to have adapted, accepted painted devils and funny faces so as now in the morning to be able to dance around Minnie, Minnie Brown, we're home again from Dungloe town, and to tell her in a pattering hail-shower of words in two voices about Donegal and the ocean and the crabs in the glass-jars and the golden and white strands of the Rosses. Soldier's Cap has been detailed to carry the crabs into the kitchen. Corkman says: Anything to keep them quiet.

He sits by the outer door, pistol in hand, back to the wall. Soldier's Cap has been sent out again to watch the world and the loaded car. Binchey Two sits on the couch, his head in his hands, brooding, his father fears, violence. The two women cook breakfast. It is Sunday morning and callers are unlikely and it is the custom of the house to pick up the Sunday papers in the town after mass. So there will be no newsboy. For all the townspeople know, they are still in Donegal.

—He's all ears, Gasmask hisses. He's one of the big ones.

—Who? That half-educated gutty from Cork. He's big when he's out like the prick of a jackass.

—Holy God, Mr. Bee, be careful. Keep your voice down.

—In my own house.

—It's his house now. For the cause. You were good to my father, Mr. Bee, my father always says.

—The son repays me.

—It's the cause, Mr. Bee. We must get the Brits out of Ireland. They want our oil.

—Our hairoil. I never knew we had oil.

—We will have offshore oil.

—You won't see much of it, Bertie boy, where you're going. You'll have more need of luck than I'll have.

—Not my name, Mr. Bee. Walls have ears. The trees outside have ears.

—You really are a poet, Bertie. Your father was a decent man. Your father's son shouldn't be mixed up in this.

—I'm a soldier of the Republic.

—You're an ass. You could give me that gun. Mad Eyes Minahan has only a knife.

—Jesus, Mr. Bee, you know him too.

—No mask could hide those mad eyes.

He hadn't recognised the eyes. He had just guessed. If I survive this, will I pass the names to the police?

Carefully he knots his dark-green tie, Dublin poplin. He could do with a clean shirt: and suddenly his care for such things at such a time seems crazily comic. Yet he dusts the broad shoulders of his pin-striped jacket, carefully polishes and sets his pince-nez: she had always liked them.

—You could give me that gun.

—Dear God, Mr. Bee, talk sense. You were a teacher. He'd kill us all. Even if he didn't get me, they would. There's no way out. Sorry, Mr. Bee.

The elbow of his left arm, slightly crooked, pains a little as it has done most mornings since he broke it in a boxing bout in college and, after my time, my son was shaping well on the college team but he lost interest and gave all his heart to farming: and perhaps Bertie, as stupid as his father before him, is right and there's no way out, and Corkman is calling from the kitchen to say that time is ticking away and the milk may be boiled over.

His son still sits with his head in his hands. The empty doll's pram is under the table. The doll is asleep in Minnie's bed. The crabs stare out from their jar on the wide windowsill. Rashers and eggs and tea laced with brandy, good for the ticking of the heart. There's a double naggin of brandy in the back of the car and he hopes they haven't found out about that. The family sit and eat, and Corkman and Bertie guard the doors, they'll eat, Corkman says, when the milk is safely on the road. His son's strong hands, now marmalading bread for the children, are matted with dark hair, none on his head, the fingers are thick and flat-tipped, brutal. He is dangerously silent. Could have been a champion in the ring but it was nature for him to find his content on the land, among cattle and horses, behind him generations of strong

farmers who had survived the famine of the 1840s and grown
stronger in a new and better world. Branching out into saddlery
which also belonged to the land, then into a fleet of hackney cars
which seemed to be a natural successor to saddlery. Or unnatural?
Over the tea laced with brandy, Franco-Irish courage, gallant
France, indomitable Ireland, the noble name of Hennessy, he
sniffs the wax-end and leather and daubing in the saddlery, then
the gasolene in the garages, another new world, old Ford cars, tin
lizzies, that stood high and stilted and quivered like thorough-
breds when you set the engine running, and had never been
perverted to carry bombs. Proxy or otherwise. Looking back at it
now it was a lost lyrical innocent place in which gasolene smelled
sweet as the rose and droppings of spilled gasolene reflected
all the colours of the rainbow. Corkman says: Let's take a look
at the goods.

His son's wife picks up from the floor the severed ropes and
gag, puts them in a plastic trash-bag and hopes out loud that
they'll never be used in this house again. Then sits on the couch,
her arms around her children. The little girl, golden as her
mother with the promise of wine, wears a leprechaun's navy-
blue jacket and slacks, remembers, and hides her face against her
mother and whimpers a little. It could, except for the whimpering, be an idyllic picture. They look at her in silence. But
do masks or the minds in them really look? What can they see
but other masks? Not men or women or children. Not the
shadows of God.

There is a low sky and gentle mizzling rain but a promise in the
light wind that the sun will shine before long. The red tricycle
with green wheels has somehow or other found its way out to
the yard. Lacking the sun the borders of oxalis are closed and
colourless. Bertie is a poet and the trees have ears. And the lake.

And eyes too. There it is, silent as if nothing had happened. But you can't fool me. The treacherous waves. You know what happened. You helped it to happen. The searchers in the black boats have not yet started work. Or do men search for murder weapons on the seventh day? Lough Muck, Loch no Muice, the lake of the pig. Pig's lake, what pig? *Me and Andy one evening was strolling, we were happy and gay you can bet, and when passing by Drumragh new graveyard, a young Loughmuck sailor we met.* She sleeps forever in new Drumragh on the wrong arm of the cross. *He brought us along to his liner that was breasting the lake like a duck. And that was the start of our ill-fated cruise on the treacherous waves of Loughmuck.* That now was the first verse of the comic song: two drunks from the town astray in these rural parts, falling footless in a dyke, suffering alcoholic comas about an ocean cruise on the oval inland lake, a comic laughing lake, sea-lions, sharks, alligators, whales, shipwreck, and a pity it was that the name of death, *oh the sights that we saw as we waited for death*, had to be mentioned in the chorus of the song: *There we lay on that beach quite exhausted till a man with a big dog drew near. He shouted out, Hey, clear away out of this, we want no drunk towney boys here.* Laughter and innocence were gone. The shadow of the monstrous mythological pig brooded over a landscape that could never free itself from vengeance and old wrongs. A pig of an island, an island changed by the magic of the Tuatha-de-Danaan into that mammoth of a black pig crouching on the sea, so as to try to prevent the Milesian wandering heroes from coming safely to haven on their isle of destiny. What a destiny, to consort with murderers in the valley of the black pig.

Corkman opens the boot of the car which has been reversed or pushed back to the hayshed, in which there is another car, a Ford Cortina. But it didn't come there during the night. No noise. Must have been there before we drove from the happiness of Donegal into the haunted farmyard.

—You're a learned man, Corkman says.

Bertie, like a statue of the Rifleman, stands in the shrubbery away at the gable of the house.

—There she is. You'll like to know what's in her.

She is a stout squat creamery can, shining silver.

—One hundred pounds of ammonium nitrate mixed with fuel oil and about three pounds of gelignite.

—A sweet cocktail.

—She'll do the job. Watch her. Technologically we've made big advances.

Carefully he closes the boot: Don't bump her, old man.

—Advances? Towards what?

—That's the way we'll bugger the Brits. Technology.

The town hall, the post office, any innocent person who might be in them or walking the street past them, Judge Flynn doomed because of his virtue: a madman spoke behind the mask, the man in the mask was mad.

—Some American says that shortly any fool will be able to make a hydrogen bomb in his own backyard.

—You read too much, old man.

Once upon a time a creamery can had been a harmless or lovely, even a musical object. Up and down the street in the town in which he was reared, the horses and carts from the farms would travel, bright with jingling cans, taking fresh milk to the creamery, taking away the skim milk for cattlefood. In Hamilton's smithy where three gigantic Presbyterian men, a father and two sons, swung their hammers and reddened the forge, the horses and the cartwheels were shod when the need arose: Presbyterian iron, and across the street his father and his helpers, all Catholics, including Bertie's poor fool of a father, provided the leather.

Genuine co-operation: the horses had no sectarian prejudices. One large red-faced farmer-boy would sit sideways on his cart, outsized hobnailed feet trailing the ground and, fancying himself perhaps on the Oregon trail, would sing in the rural dialect: Rowl along, covered wagon, rowl along.

No shuddering shattering death in those bright cans.

Nowadays motor-trucks took the cans to a modern factory.

—Time's ticking away, Corkman says.

He agrees. What else is new? Corkman is a bore: and suddenly the brutal effrontery of the whole business freezes his blood and sets him shivering. What right have these brainless bastards with their half-baked ideas to crash in on the lives of better people, to bind and gag old women, set children whimpering, and himself bearing death and ruin to the town he loves. Ireland? What Ireland? Ulster? What Ulster? Multiplying like body-lice, the other crabs, in the hairy undergrowth, one madman produces another. He says to Corkman that, indeed, time is ticking away, that they're all closer to the grave than they were yesterday morning. He says: I heard of a man who defied a gang like you . . .

—Gang? Watch it, old man.

—And said: Murder me now. What would you do, Corkman?

—Try me and see. Nobody would miss your son, for starters. But listen to me now and listen good and no codacting. You can't take the short way into the town. They may be easy on a Sunday morning at the roadblock but you might bump her on the ramps. She's as delicate as a virgin.

Then the backdoor of the house slams thunderously. Soldier's Cap has come backwards out through the doorway like a rocket and is flat on his ass and roaring. Bertie the imbecile, soldier of the legion of the rearguard like his father before him, is also flat but on his belly, shotgun aimed on the backdoor. Corkman says:

Don't move, old man. Charlie Chaplin couldn't guard a henhouse. Has farmer boy a gun?

—He has the 'phone.

—It's small use to him. We fixed that. Be your age. Has he a gun?

—He has a shotgun somewhere.

—In the house?

Soldier's Cap rises, falls again over the green-wheeled red tricycle, comes crawling crabwise across the yard towards the hayshed and his master and the loaded car and the concealed can. Corkman calmly raises the pistol: Jesus, I could shoot him where he creeps. Only it wouldn't be worth the noise. The dung I have to work with. Where's the shotgun, old man?

Soldier's Cap crawls closer. Bertie leaps to his feet and, in a perfect imitation of a British paratrooper shooting down civilians in Derry on Bloody Sunday, races round the corner of the house, goes down, shotgun ready, on one knee, under a window-sill and close to the backdoor. Bertie has studied the art of war, or whatever it is, on the teevee.

—You may as well spill, old man. It's not in the house.

He may as well spill. His son hasn't a hope. He says: No shooting then. If so, no driving. The gun's up on hooks in the stable-loft.

—It's safe there. We'll get it later. And no conditions, old man. Who in hell do you think is boss around here?

Soldier's Cap has crawled into what he thinks is the shelter of the hayshed. He moans what seems to mean that his jaw is broken. He rises to his knees: and, fair enough, if his jaw isn't broken it, and his mask, are in some disarray: my son still has a good right, and it is mad Minahan. Then Corkman with care and deliberation kicks Soldier's Cap in the privates and the creature goes down again howling.

—A lesson in discipline, soldier. And now, old man. Into battle.

The pistol is pressed against the back of his head.

—Walk slowly across to within twenty paces of the door. Tell the idiot farmer boy to step out backwards, hands behind back. Women and children in kitchen and quiet. If not I'll shoot you in one knee-cap. Also we'll run the milk delivery up the back-door and leave it there. Time's ticking away. The virgin's in the boot. Waiting to be bust. Fed-up fooling, old man. Soldier-boy on your feet. You stupid fucker. The Battle of Britain and Paddy Finnucane. And get the cuffs out of the Cortina.

He stirs mad Minahan more than briskly with his foot and the creature rises and hobbles, doubled-up and moaning, towards the hidden car. They pace across the yard. Quasimodo Minahan lurches behind. The borders of oxalis are stirring in expectation of the sun. The birds are busy. The birds sang around Dachau. The mouth of the pistol is not touching his head but he feels that it is. Cold shivering anger at outrage is not enough. You need guns and bombs and swinging ropes and the shooting of hostages. But here and now there's no help for it, no way out. If the milk has to be delivered anywhere, better not at your own door. So his son steps out backwards, hands behind his back, and Quasimodo, hobbling sideways and groaning, snaps the cuffs on him in a flash and a click and, for better value, kicks him viciously on the shins. Corkman laughs again that astoundingly good-natured laugh and says: Chained in the market-place he stood, a man of giant frame

Then: To the wheel, old man, to the wheel.

—Will my son be safe?

The humiliation, oh heart of Jesus, the humiliation, hoors, whores and worms.

—If he minds himself, and if you deliver the goods. He can't masturbate the way he is. He won't grow hair on the palms of his hands To the wheel, old man.

—The women? My daughter-in-law? The children?

Bertie's father's awkward feet have walked into the house.

—No time, old man, for tearful farewells. Kiss them all you want when you come back. If you ever do. Time's ticking away.

The pistol, really touching his head, pushes him towards the car. His son stands silent, chained in the market-place amid the gathering multitude that shrank to hear his name, men without hands, girls without legs in restaurants in Belfast, images of Ireland Gaelic and free, never till the latest day shall the memory pass away of the gallant lives thus given for our land, images of Ulster or of a miserable withdrawn corner of O'Neill's Irish Ulster safe from popery and brass money and wooden shoes. These mad dogs have made outrage a way of life. To the wheel, to the wheel, to the wheel, time's ticking away, in the town the churchbells are ringing, Catholic, Church of Ireland, Presbyterian, Methodist, Baptist, all calling people away from each other to get them in the end by various routes, *variis itineribus* to the home in the heavens of the same omnipotent, omniscient, omnipresent Great Father with a long white beard, but why not unite here and now and not wait for then, come all to church good people good people come and pray, and the angel of death is at the wheel or on the wing, and ye know neither the day nor the hour.

Before him like a blood-red flag the bright flamingoes flew. The bright evil lake is behind him. The car runs well. To look at it, nobody would have a notion. This now is the crossroads and the longest way round is the shortest way home. And his still-silent, silvery passenger, glutted with fuel oil and gelignite and ammonium nitrate, might be discommoded into burping by the bumps

of the ramps. Beloved, may your sleep be sound. She sleeps in
New Drumragh. Death sleeps in the silver can. In Dublin long
ago he had gone with her to see that movie about Venezuela and
the wages of fear. A friend of his had even introduced them
to the Frenchman who had written the novel: a tall man, visiting
Dublin at the time, who wrote about dead-beats in a vile South
American town, island of lost souls, taking perilous jobs, only
the lost would take them, that was a pothole and a bad bump,
driving nitroglycerine or something to mines or quarries or was
it oil-wells: the occupational hazard, a blinding flash over the
ridge, scarcely an explosion, just a blinding flash and that
was that.

But at least those wrecks of men were paid to carry the stuff.
More or less they went willingly. If they won through they had
their ticket to somewhere out of hell. If they didn't, they felt
no more pain While I ferry murder to my town and its people
so as to save my children, my children's children, an old deserted
woman, a long white house. And on the cause must go, through
joy or weal or woe, till we make Ireland a nation free and grand.
Not even the Mafia thought of the proxy bomb, operation proxy,
proxopera for gallant Irish patriots fighting imaginary empires by
murdering the neighbours. Could Pearse in the post office have,
by proxy, summoned Cuchulain to his side, could the wild geese
have, by proxy, spread the grey wing on the bitter tide, could
all that delirium of the brave not have died by proxy, Edward
Fitzgerald, and Robert Emmet and Wolfe Tone? Corkman
seemed semi-educated, and must know that poem, and also,
let me carry your cross for Ireland, Lord, but let some other
unfortunate fucker carry the bomb for me.

Proxopera, he says, and likes the sound of the word.

Proxopera Binchey, fit foe for the Red Baron, zooming in to
attack, and dear God there was a bump that nearly stopped my

faulty heart, my palms are sweating, my crotch is scourged and where in God's name is the brandy that was under the cushion in the back of the car? He finds it, and blessed be God, blessed be His holy name and blessed forever be the holy name of Hennessy, and stands on the roadway sipping, and breathing in the living morning. This is a quiet place, and a good place to drive the accursed thing into a field and be shut of it forever, except that he knows that some of them, not Corkman, not Bertie, not mad Minahan, but some fourth monster, and unmasked and like an ordinary human being, is watching him from somewhere, hedgerow, hilltop, to see does he truly deliver the goods.

Six weeks ago that man near Kesh, by the Erne in County Fermanagh, was ordered to take a loaded bomb into the town and simply drove it at sixty into a field and jumped out and scuttled for his life and the gunmen took off in panic, like shit off a shovel, in his car and didn't stop for twenty miles and abandoned his car beyond Ballyshannon: real true Irish heroes, they were, when their own yellow hides were in peril. Like the way they were all to stand and fight if the Brits went ahead with Operation Motorman and went into the Bogside in Derry, but on the day and night of Operation Motorman the heroes were safe across the Border getting heroically drunk in Bundoran on the ocean, a health resort of high renown. But at Kesh there were no hostages: and what would that Corkman and mad Minahan do to his son and his wife and children: soldiers of the Republic in their own eyes, knee-cappers, murderers, arsonists, protection racketeers, decorators of young girls with tar and feathers, God, the oddities that in times like these crawled out from under the stones.

The green rolling landscape is happy all around him. Where are the watchers hiding?

* * *

Brandy breaks out in sweat on his brow. Time's ticking away. He's as lonely as Alexander Selkirk, lord of the fowl and the brute, lord of destruction and the day of doom. Into battle then. To the wheel. To the wheel. Get a good grip on myself. Another sip. More sweat, but the heart seems easy. A man of my age in Belfast was forced to drive a bomb to the Europa hotel, already bombed seventeen times, and had a heart attack and died, and the bomb didn't even go off: the cursed murderous cretins, and all the happy days I passed along this road on my way to the innocent lake and the vision of the white house of destiny: and now, out of humanity's reach, I Alexander Selkirk, on my own island and passing her holy grave without time for a prayer, must finish my journey alone.

Traffic is slight for a Sunday morning. Have the men of blood frightened the people from going to mass or meeting? Three cars overtake him and hoot at him in salute, and in the noise and reverberation of their passing he grips the wheel until his sweating palms hurt. He doesn't hoot back. They'll all be surprised to see me driving. God preserve any of them from stopping to make enquiries. An old woman – oddly enough he doesn't recognise her although he thought he knew everybody on this road – thumbs a lift and, out of habit, he is almost about to respond. She'll be amazed and annoyed that he hasn't. People in these parts were always generous about giving lifts. These morons have blighted the landscape, corrupted custom, blackened memory, drawn nothing from history but hatred and poison. Proxopera, proxopera lift up your voice and sing. So he sings, but softly: Going to mass last Sunday my true love passed me by. I knew her mind was altered by the rolling of her eye. And when I stood in God's dark light, my tongue could word no prayer, knowing my saint had fled and left her reliquary bare.

My true love passed me by. No, but I passed her by, in fear and without a prayer, when I passed the green spiked railings of new Drumragh. He sings again, this is as close to prayer as I can come: Ringleted youth of my love with your bright golden tresses behind thee, you passed on the road up above but you never came in to find me.

How dear to me now, doomed to solitude, a murderer by proxy, are my memories, how dear the ordinary details of life, a red tricycle with green wheels, a doll's pram, the rocks of Donegal, two crabs in a glass jar, the wrinkled face of an old woman, the winy body of a young woman, the bald head of my angry son, the voices of his children, the sound of the hooves of his horses, the oxalis opening to the sun now breaking out splendidly beyond my doomed town.

Spiked green railings surround the dead, the gravelled cross divides them.

Outside a Wesleyan hall in Belfast a woman has been found impaled on the railings. Foul play is not suspected. She fell from a window. Of a Wesleyan hall? Odd, very odd. And in Belfast, where for six years there has been nothing but foul play. Christ, there I went bump bump over a bridge over a small stream out of which, with the humble worm, I took my first ever brown trout. Has the creamery can moved? Rattled? How do you fall from the window of a Wesleyan hall and impale yourself on the railings? Shades of Shaka, the great Zulu, who amused himself by seating his enemies on pointed stakes and letting them sink to find their own level. A very painful happening, buggery by proxy, proxbuggery. But the Turks had more finesse with a slender, pliable, tough rod tapped gently in at the anus and up and up, an expert job, and out at the back of the neck and one end of the rod lashed securely to the other and the victim raised on a pole to perish as soon or as slowly as he pleased. With their hammers and nails and carpentered crosses the ancient Romans were a crude bloody crowd. Proxopera in the highest, hosanna to the king.

Long ago she said in all innocence: Take my cherry.

They were sitting in an ice-cream parlour in O'Connell Street in Dublin.

He picked the cherry from the top of her phallic Bombe Cardinale, blunted multi-coloured obelisk of ice-cream, and told her what she had just said, and she blushed and laughed and laughed and blushed, and still I remember the first touch of the tip of my finger on the fragile membrane.

—She's as delicate, Corkman said, as a virgin.

Or was that what the bastard had said?

And that, God above, was another bad bump. St. Christopher, pray for me, who carried Christ on your back, I carry Lucifer, evil and a blinding light.

Once in an old churchyard that must have been in some eighteenth-century engraving, and beside a high Norman earthwork, a friend of mine and myself came on a Sunday on a newly-opened grave, opened to receive its guest on the Monday morning. Down, deep-down in the next door grave reposed a skeleton, not a bone out of place, but bed-clothes temporarily disturbed for the reception of the new guest. Inlaid to the brown clay, head tilted restfully back, hands joined together a little above where manhood or membrane might have been. She sleeps for the life of the world in new Drumragh where soon, perhaps, I may join her but, also perhaps, not with my bones in their proper positions. Before the city hall in Belfast people kneel around more than a thousand small white crosses, one cross for every person murdered in the name of Ireland or the name of Protestant Ulster. Bertie of the blundering hereditary feet talks of the

Republic, Corkman the crazy talks of technology, and I drive on, sick with fear and an awful resignation, to bring death to my own, to keep death from my own.

My father was a great man for bananas, treaclebread and oatmeal porridge. Three hundred and sixty-five days of the year, three hundred and sixty-six in Leap Year, even on Christmas day and after the Christmas dinner, he would prepare and sup his own oatmeal.

Once upon a time the country people held that human skulls had healing properties, chiefly for the healing of epilepsy. You broke off a little bit of the skull, ground it into powder and drank it. That is, if you were an epileptic. Also, milk could be boiled in the skull and given to the patient. Over there near Keadue on the shores of Lough Key in the west of Ireland, the skull of Turlough O'Carolan, the last of the bards, was so used until somebody stole it from his tomb. To preserve the bard's skull? Or to make a corner in the curing of epilepsy? In new Drumragh she sleeps forever, her skull on a pillow and under a canopy of Ulster clay. Goldsmith, Thackeray said, could have heard O'Carolan and God of Almighty what am I thinking of, broken-down pedant sitting on a volcano, Empedocles on Aetna, and that was a bump and a bump and an 'alf and my hands are so slippy they can hardly hold the wheel till the vessel strikes with a shivering shock, even the roads have gone to blazes since the troubles began, Good Heavens it is the Inchcape Rock, as our ship glided over the water we all gazed at the landscape we knew, we passed Clanabogan's big lighthouse and the Pigeon Top faded from view: but, alas, as we sped o'er the waters, we were all soon with horror dumbstruck, for without any warning a big storm arose on the treacherous waves of Lough Muck, and Sacred Heart of Jesus what now is happening in my white house that I first saw and loved across the waters of the lake that have been polluted forever: and Bertie's father was a born fool for this night, when my father was cooking the porridge, he steps into our kitchen with a collection box, and all round his left bicep a tricoloured ribbon oh, collecting cash for Caithlin Ni Houlihan, the Hag of Beare and Caith Ni Dhuibhir, and Patrick Pearse and the sainted dead who died for Ireland. Nowadays people die for Ireland in the oddest ways.

—And what will you do with the money, says my father and he carefully watching the bubbling oatmeal.

—Elect members to Stormont and Westminster, Mr. Binchey.

—And what will you do then, Brian boy?

—The members will then abstain from attendance, Mr. Binchey. They'll be abstentionist members.

—Bully for them. That'll save train and boatfare. And what will you do then, Brian?

—Spread our propaganda among the Orangemen, Mr. Binchey. Bring them round to our way of thinking.

—A laudable intention. And what then, Brian?

—Declare a republic, Mr. Binchey.

—Oh la dee da, says my father and goes on stirring the porridge.

But how could Brian help it and the way he was reared, with an uncle that was forever in and out of jail for Ireland and an aunt that blew herself up making bombs for Ireland and a mother that ran a restaurant and lodging-house always as full of republicans as Rome before the Caesars, so that it was regularly being raided by the Royal Ulster Constabulary, and one night Brian's mother and Bertie's grandmother poured from a second-floor window, and all for Ireland, the contents of a chamber-pot from under the bed of a drunken journeyman-carpenter, over the shoulders of a police sergeant who came knock knocking at the

door: and the sergeant's name was Poxy Thompson because of
the pock marks on his face and for no worse reason, and one of
his shoulders was lower or higher than the other. A family that
was fierce Irish, as they'd say in irony in Dublin, and now Bertie
on his father's feet and with a face like a faceless monster goes
plodding unbidden around the house of my boyhood dreams.

But Kyrie Eleison what is this on the road on a Sunday morning,
smoke rising from the smouldering stump of what's left of the
Orange Hall where once that love-bewildered young Protestant
provoked a riot by footing the light fantastic with a papist girl.
In this present Ulster world there's little place for the light
fantastic: close to Newry town the U.V.F. or was it the U.D.A.
murdered a showband.

My road drops down, doing a double bend, into a saucer of
a valley. High, green, terraced banks, no turn left or right,
no turning back, no way out except straight through: *There we
were like two Robinson Crusoes far away from Fireagh Orange Hall.
Though we starved on that rock for a fortnight, not a ship ever came
within call.* Fireagh, here I come. And the Orange Hall has just
gone. Up in smoke. Thirty or so people are in and around what's
left of it. As close to the smouldering ruins as they dare to go. The
flames have blackened the bushes on the high bank above. Sweet
sight for a Sunday in a good autumn. No soldiers around. This is a
fire. Not a fight. Thank God for that. But for what? One policeman
raises his blue-black arm. What can I do but stop? No use to say to
him halt me at your peril. And the peril of everybody in this little
valley. And of my son and his wife and Gary and Catherine and
Minnie, Minnie Brown we're home again from Dungloe town.

—Good morning, Mr. Binchey. Bit of a surprise to see you at
the wheel.

A decent fellow. I drank with his father. Also in the force.

And a brother of his, a plain-clothes man, murdered in the town, twelve months ago. Sitting reading the paper at a barcounter when two gunmen walked in. Into a pub in which he had had his first drink. And in which on my way from teaching I used to drink with his father, at the same counter at the same place. Tried to pull his gun. They shot him once. Crawled into the gents. They followed him and finished the job and shouted: We have you in the right place on the shithouse floor.

That pub would never be the same again.

—Good morning, constable. I wouldn't be at the wheel only necessity knows no law.

How true, how bloody true.

—We got back from Donegal last night. Margaret wasn't feeling too well. Robert's on the suspended list. As you know. So old grandad has to head off to the chemist. But I'm taking it easy.

—It's the best thing to do these days, Mr. Binchey. If you can. What do you think of that on a Sunday morning?

The engine purrs. He's afraid to cut it off. God only knows what restarting might do. The constable is a squat solid civil fellow with a squint, and his face smudged from the fire the way the soldiers, now and in this place, smudge their faces on night patrol, in my own town, dear God, battledress and camouflage in my own town. Could I tell him that time is ticking away? Could I tell him that someone in the crowd is watching?

—What happened, constable?

—I.R.A. I'd say, a reprisal for the Catholic Church at Altamuskin. The U.V.F. tossed a bomb into that.

—Oh, what a wonderful war.

—So now the U.V.F. will bomb another Catholic church. Or a Catholic pub. Then the I.R.A. will shoot a policeman or bomb a Protestant pub. And then the U.V.F . . .

—Was the brigade here?

—Couldn't make it. Fires everywhere this bloody morning. All a few miles outside town. Cornstacks. Barns. Anything.

Aha, the grand strategy, get the brigade away from the town, make straight the path for Binchey the Burner. Time's ticking away.

—They could be up to something else, Mr. Binchey. All this could be a diversion.

It sure as God could, except that diversion is not the word that Mr. Binchey, his ass squelching in a pool of sweat, his stomach frozen with fear, his mind running crazily on irrelevancies, would have chosen. What at the moment is relevant? Time's ticking away. Time's relevant. How long have I left? How long has anybody left? Half an hour after I place the bomb even at the remoter place, the Judge's house, say fifty minutes to an hour, constable, constable let me pass or I'll wet my pants or my heart will stop.

—These are queer times, Mr. Binchey, pubs and churches, women and children, my own brother, the Tower of London, and in London too the Ideal Homes Exhibition, a bomb by the escalator, sixty-five mutilated and eleven of them Irish, bad, mad times.

With utterly resigned terror Mr. Binchey recalls that the constable's father was an amiable long-winded man. In the smouldering wreckage another constable has discovered something and the crowd has gathered around him. So if I go up I'll only bring this boy with me. The watcher, whoever he is, will be watching from a safe distance. That's the name of the game. Proxopera. Proxopera. He spells it to himself as a sort of charm to move the man to let him pass. But, hands on the door of the car, stooping down, square head half in the window, smudged face still smelling of good aftershave lotion, the young man in blue-black uniform one of the last surviving symbols of an empire gone forever into the shadows, is prepared to talk to Mr. Binchey, as venerable, as respectable, as comforting as the face of the town clock: this is an historic moment and I was a teacher of history and Latin and English literature, and time is ticking away.

—But one of the worst things of all, Mr. Binchey, was that business in the Catholic graveyard at Lisnagarda on the outskirts of Scarva in County Down. Even in the bloody graveyard nothing's sacred.

She sleeps, waiting for me, in new Drumragh, I come, I come, my heart's delight.

—I didn't hear about that.

—It happened, I'd say, when you were in Donegal. The care-taker of the graveyard, sixty-one years of age, a woman, walking in the graveyard in the morning, sees a wreath lying on the path. Purple plastic chrysanthemums and white roses. Thinks it was blown from a new grave. Picks it up. Boom. Boobytrapped. Sure as Jesus. Could you beat that, Mr. Binchey?

An awkward question, in the silvery can, constable my constable, time is ticking away, I'm booby-trapped like the white roses and purple plastic chrysanthemums, we may boom and go aloft together.

—Only a part of it went off or the poor woman was done for. As it was, hands, legs and body severely injured. An old lady. Sixty-one. In a consecrated graveyard. Blood running out of her, she staggered three hundred yards to the nearest cottage, rapped on the window and collapsed. Only one shoe and stocking on, blood everywhere. Something, she said, hit me on the foot when I lifted the wreath. God in heaven, wouldn't you think an old woman would be safe in a graveyard?

Every spring we lay on her grave a bunch of daffodils, a branch of green and golden whin.

—Nothing's sacred, Mr Binchey. But I'd better not hold you up. You'd better not indeed.

—And the odd thing, Mr Binchey, is that a lot of these fellows, IRA or UVF or UDA, or ABCDEXYZ, if left alone wouldn't hurt a cat or a child. But get a few of them together and give them what they think is a leader or an ideal and they'd destroy Asia and themselves and their nearest and dearest.

A military truck comes from the direction of the town.

—Good luck, Mr Binchey. And I hope young Mrs Binchey will be well soon.

—Thank you, constable. And so do I.

Two soldiers walk towards them. They wave casually at Mr Binchey as he goes on his way towards the town he was reared in.

Those two soldiers looked like lizards, protective colouring to be worn in the emerald isle, Ireland of the welcomes and the bomb in the pub and the bullet in the back. He remembers a time when the soldiers in the town dressed smartly, pipeclayed belts and shining brass badges, polished nailed boots, puttees rolled with precision, peaked caps at an exact angle, walking cane under the oxter the way you'd truss a chicken. They were part of the town then, too, even if they were also part of the far-flung empire: the Royal Irish, the Royal Inniskillings, the pipes playing Adieu to Bellashanny and the Inniskilling Dragoon as they marched from the barracks to the railway station and thence to Aldershot and India or Egypt or the West Indies or Hong Kong or the Burma Road itself. A soldier out for the evening could talk to friends on the street although regulations did not encourage them to loiter at street corners. They drank with the people in the pubs and no madman gloried in shooting them dead in the shithouse. They relaxed with the girls in and around a public park. Or, better still, in whatever private place a poor man could find. Nobody thought of them as an invading hostile army. No girl had her head shaved or was tarred and feathered.

But then we always had with us Bertie's father and the like of him.

Curious thing, but the only book I ever saw in the hands of Bertie's father was a copy of *Mein Kampf*. Not in his hands exactly, but under the oxter where the soldiers kept the canes. He had a stiff left leg and always wore a brown belted overcoat, and had no brains, and through 1939 and 1940 he was never without that book. Never did I see him open it to peek at the treasures within. Was he like the vagrant who was washed and treated at a delousing centre and was delighted to discover, buried under alluvial mud in his navel, a collar-stud he had lost six years before? Yet he carried, even if he didn't read, *Mein Kampf*, because since the Jerries were marching against and going to invade England, Hitler had to be a republican. Declare a republic, Mr. Binchey. Oh la dee da, says my father, and goes on stirring the porridge. And about the same time there was a crazy missionary father going around, a roaring beanpole of a man, preaching missions in rural and even urban churches, the purest Goebbels who had noebbels at all, and all about the Jews and the Freemasons, and the real names of the rulers of Russia, all ending in ski, until his religious superiors had to put a stop to his gallop and lock him up or something. Oh never fear for Ireland, boys, for she has soldiers still.

No pipeclayed belts, no shining brass badges, no girls in the park, no drinks with the people in the pubs. But soldier boys like lizards on a sunny Irish Sunday against a background of scorched hedgerows and a burned-out Orange Hall, black wicked guns carried at an angle, pointing upwards, Martian antennae. They hold on to their guns as if they might rocket into space. They whistle through their teeth so as to seem carefree. Young fellows from the other island who scarcely know where they are or what they're doing here or what in hell it's all about. Their boots are dull-black, rubber-soled. They can move as quietly as cats round corners or along alleys. In the old days you could hear the clatter of the nailed boots half a mile away: evil secrecies of the world we have lived into. Forty shades of green, ironically, the green above the red, over trousers and combat jacket. And over the bullet-proof vest, a lifejacket for very dry land, and tied down back and front. But only a black beret protects the head and where have all the tin hats and helmets gone?

Christ hear us, Christ graciously hear us, I'm gripping the wheel so hard that my left arm has gone completely numb, it's not there, it's amputated, I've only one arm remaining and the road is empty and the sun bright and high and I swelch in sweat but I'll make the bridge where the railway used to be before I rest long enough to shake and rub and exercise that arm back into existence. In Jefferson County jail in Alabama there's a prisoner who's in for using an artificial arm to kill a man—like the joker who killed Miss Kilmannsegg with and for her precious golden leg. He has two artificial arms and he complains that the people who run the prison won't let him wear them so that he can't eat, shave, brush his teeth, change his clothes or clean himself after crapping: but the prison people say that if he had his arms he'd hurt somebody, and there you are, like Ulster, an insoluble problem, and my left arm now hurts like hell so it must still be there but, *exaudi nos domine*, there's the bridge around a pastoral corner, lambs on the green hills gazing at me and many a strawberry grows by the salt sea and many a ship sails the ocean, and up a slight slope, and once up there I can survey the morning smoke of my own town.

There below me as I lean on the parapet and puff and sweat and sip the last of the brandy, the blood of Hennessy the God, is the Grand Canyon of my boyhood, now a choked-up formidable dyke where weeds and wild trailing brambles have smothered the magic well at the world's end. No train will ever again go through there bringing noisy happy summer crowds to the breakers at Bundoran. The world is in wreckage and these madmen would force me to extend that wreckage to my town below, half-asleep in the valley, my town, asleep like a loved woman on a morning pillow, my town, my town, my town. Declare a republic, Mr. Binchey, destroy the town, Mr. Binchey. Who's watching me now? Where are they? And down in the Grand Canyon I ate sweet raw turnips and drank, from the rock, water as cool as Moselle. That spring will never be the same again, yet for what civilisation, my town, is now worth, we still have inherited something, we have many good memories. Now I see. Let them watch and damn them to the lowest pit.

Here where I lean, the parapet was once shattered by a runaway truck and during the repairs a boy wrote in the soft concrete the name he imagined himself by: Black Wolf. And I'm the man who was the boy who wrote Black Wolf, and the concrete hardened, as is its nature, and there the name still is, and would Black Wolf ever submit to what the madmen are now trying to force on me, and go on for the rest of his life remembering that to save his own family he had planted death in his own town which is also his family? And even if every blade of grass were an eye watching me, to hell with them, let the grass wither in the deepest Stygian pits of gloom, and blast and blind the bastards and Bertie Bigboots and Mad Minahan and that creepy half-literate Cork-man. Now I see. Mud in the eyes is a help and, more than my son and his son, or the bees in the pink oxalis, I see there my town and all its people, Orange and Green, and the post office with all its clerks and postmen and red mail vans, and the town hall and its glass dome and everybody in it – from that fine man, my friend, town clerk, or mayor, for forty-odd years, down to the decent tobacco-chewing man who swabs out the public jakes in the basement, my people, my people. Under that glass dome I played as a young man in amateur theatricals, the Coming of the Magi, the Plough and the Stars, the Shadow, God help us, of a Gunman, and the return of Professor Tim and the Monkey's Paw and the shop at Sly Corner and Look at the Heffernans, and all the talk and all the harmless posturing and laughter, my people. Hissing into a sock or something Corkman couldn't know what a town is. Even by consenting for a moment to drive this load of death I've given these rotten bastards some sort of a devil's right over the lives of my people. What, after my death, will they say about me in the local papers, what would they remember: that I carried a bomb on a sunny Sunday to the town hall and the post office or to the door of Judge Flynn who's one of the best men in the north and who goes every day in danger: they've already murdered a good Judge at his door in the morning and in the presence of his seven-year-old daughter, and now I see and there she is, the virgin, the sleeping beauty inaccessible in a sleeping wood, and thorns and thorns around her and the cries of night? Did she stir in her sleep? Did her guts rumble? My left arm stings but it is alive again.

He places his left hand, palm flat, on the creamery can. He strokes her as if she were a cat. He recalls harmless tricks of boyhood, putting carbide in tins, boring holes in the tins, clamping down the lids, dripping water through the holes, listening for the hiss, putting matches to the holes, and delighting in the bangs and the soaring tins: or tossing squibs over the garden fences of crabbed old men. Down in the valley his town

is at peace and blue peace is on the hills beyond. This may
be farewell forever, the end of my ill-fated cruise on the treacherous waves of Lough Muck. He says to the can that, daughter of
Satan, you'll never get to where you were sent. The beleaguered
white house is far away in another world, her grave is very
near. He closes the boot carelessly, turns the car sharply on the
road, and drives back towards the nameless lake of the mad
old women.

That pillar of smoke, of cloud, ahead of me cannot, surely to
God, be still coming from the corpse of the Orange Hall. The
smoke had died down before I left the place. Where does it come
from? Up the steep hill and into the tunnel of tall beeches. Not
yet russet enough to make the road seem warm. Up and down
this hill, through this tunnel, walked so often that amazing
family of strong, red-cheeked, flaxen-haired brothers and sisters,
a dozen or more of them, clutching their bibles and meditating,
perhaps, on Lot's daughters and the night before. All gone
now. Where to? Somewhere in England? Lost in the last war?
Did they separate or stay together? House and place went to
a stronger farmer who lives elsewhere. The house, a barn now
like the barns behind it, and out of the tunnel and close to
the hilltop and the checkpoint Charley and, under God, it's
the barns are on fire, not smoke only but fine dancing flames,
another diversion, all the fun of the fair, to keep the army and
police away from Binchey the Bomber! They'd burn all Ireland
so as I could plant one bomb to burn what was left and get
the Brits on the run. Who'd want to stay? The Irish have to.
Some of them.

Only two soldiers, lizards, at the checkpoint. One looking one
way, one another, for the enemy, for fire-bugs, for the brigade if
it ever gets here.

Careful and slow, the ramp might bust the virgin.

So he says to one soldier, and is amazed at the cold steadiness of his own voice, many an old woman walked along this road to a lonely end: There's a bomb in this car, I want to dump it in the bog beyond, proxopera, a proxy bomb.

The first soldier says: Fuck.

Involuntarily goes back a step.

The second soldier says: Let me take the wheel, dad.

The first soldier says: I'll phone the squad. Is gone.

—The wheel, dad.

—Why should you? It isn't your town.

—Hurry, dad.

—They have my house and family. The white house by the lake.

—Dad.

—Follow me. Keep far away.

He drives on. More rapidly. Fuck: to quote the first soldier.

Far behind he hears the siren of the brigade. Fuck, again. What does it matter? This road that I drive on is Suicide Road. Wages of fear. Many an old woman. Now an old, an aging, man. Dad, indeed. Grandad. A boy walked along this road to see a vision of his white house. Up and down on esker land, sandy humps, that the icebergs left behind. The lake is below, bog birch and sally bushes, nobody ever fished there, nothing there ever but death, the still water glistens, shimmers, dances, for a moment he sees two lakes, then one lake as large as the ocean, boundaries fading and undefined. Now here, where old withered women stumbled to meet the dark lover, should, surely to Satan, be the place for the virgin to awake, relax, open legs, abandon the membrane. A dry season, thank God, and wheels don't sink on the turf-cutter's path that goes through bog and birches, but bump, bump, bump, he goes, and branches crack against the windows and sides of the car and on and on, and why not now go on and on and the spirits of old dead women, with such hair too, shriek around him. The car stops. The front wheels sink. That's that. Out and away. Which way? To the lake? The road is back there, and the soldiers, some of them, he hears coming carefully after him. He, carefully also, goes towards them, not stumbling. It's not over. Every step is a step towards the white house. The harvest colours are splendid on the hills above and around the bog. Beech leaves will soon begin to redden. He walks between two soldiers. And the elder of Lot's daughters said to the younger: Come let us make him drunk with wine and let us lie with him that we may preserve the seed of our father, for our father is old, and there is no man left on the earth to come in unto us after the manner of the whole earth.

A voice, the second soldier, says: Dad, you're raving. Shock.

Somewhere behind there's a muffled boom. His feet are on the hard road. Strong arms are holding him.

—Let me see. Now I see.

They turn him round. The pillar of cloud rises out of the bog, birches and sally bushes. There's some flame and crackling. Judge Flynn is at home. The town goes about its Sunday business. He tells them about the old women who committed suicide in that nameless lake. The first soldier says effing lucky you weren't a suicide yourself.

—Careful, dad, says the second soldier. Here, lean on me.

There's a crowd on the road, around a Land Rover.

—All this, says the first soldier, is what my dad used to call a real Irish fuck-up. My dad, you see, was Irish, from Liverpool.

But the only thing he can see is a grainfield, red for the reaper. Beyond it somewhere is a white house.

—Home, he says.

—Careful, dad, says the second soldier. Some of us are on the way. You need a rest.

—Good news this morning, Mr. Binchey. Two of them blew themselves up in a car driving into the town of Keady. A loaded handgun was found in the wreckage of the car and police deduced that the men, one already dead in the garden of a roadside house . . .

You're nearer God's heart in a garden.

. . . and the second dying in the wreckage, had either been on their way to leave the bomb in Keady or to deliver it to someone else.

—The police could be correct in their deductions.

—When they go out to harm other people it's always to me a happy sight to see the harm come back to their own doors. God is just.

—Or to their own cars, Minnie. Or to other people's gardens. Once upon a time we used to talk of misguided youths.

—Who guided them or misguided them?

—Ireland. A long history. England. Empire. King William. The Pope. Ian Paisley. Myself. I was a teacher of history.

—With all due respect, Mr. Binchey, we all had the same history. How many people now in your time did you blow up and you as good an Irishman as the next?

—Two weeks ago I came close to it.

—But you didn't do it. You were a hero.

The treetops billow around his third-floor window, three shades of green, beeches turning russet. Through gaps made now and again by the billowing he glimpses a bright suburban road, a bend of a river, a bridge, his town, Venice, for the present preserved.

From the white house and the lakeshore Minnie Brown has come to him with fruit and flowers and the Sunday papers from Dublin and London: his son and daughter-in-law and grandchildren will follow later. The newspapers are filled with the most wonderful reading for an ageing man whose heart is not in the best condition. The crabs from Donegal are still alive and seemingly doing well. Minnie has survived the rascals and the blackguards and her long wrinkled face has the glow of a girl. A forty-eight-year-old father of six children, ranging in age from six to thirteen, has been killed instantly when gunmen burst into his brother's pub at Aughamullen on the shores of Lough Neagh and sprayed the public bar with bullets. The dead man is Patrick Falls, a chemist and a native of the area, but he has been residing in Birmingham for the past four years. He had previously a pharmacy business in Belfast, for sixteen years, but was forced to go to England when his shop was destroyed in an explosion. He had returned to his native Aughamullen a week previously to make arrangements for the building of a house for his wife and family and himself. On the night of his murder he had gone into the bar to allow his brother, Joseph, to have a tea-break. Only one customer was in the public bar when the gunmen entered. One of them killed Mr. Falls instantly. A second opened fire on the customer, seventy-year-old Alphonsus Quinn of Ardboe, wounding him in the arm. The gunmen fled to a waiting car and sped off in the direction of the Protestant area of Tamnamore . . .

Home is the sailor, home from the sea . . .

But on the other hand . . .

A sixteen-year-old boy who moved to Australia from Glasgow with his parents eight years ago has been murdered in rugged country near Adelaide. Police say the boy was clubbed to death. His body was found lying beside his new car. His father said the family had left Glasgow to escape violence in the streets.

And thus the whole round earth is every way bound by the gold chains about the feet of God.

—Now here's a hussy and a half, says Minnie.

She reads slowly, pointing, peering, asking for help with the more rugged words: Susan Shaw is the blonde who puts sheer enjoyment into Manikin cigars. Her abundant sex appeal has helped advertise everything from car-polish to riding saddles. She has nakedly graced the pages of the popular press . . .

—Look at her, Mr. Binchey, tearing her shirt off and her mouth open. No wonder the world is the way it is.

Mr. Binchey looks and is not displeased and makes no verbal comment. But to please Minnie he clucks a little.

—She gets twelve pounds a picture with her clothes on and two hundred and fifty in her pelt. Mr. Binchey, did you ever?

—Never, says Mr. Binchey.

Surprisingly Minnie, who hasn't much respect for sex, laughs until the tears flow down the gullies of her cheeks.

Well now, says Mr. Binchey.

His father might have said: Boysaboys.

Or Ladeeda.

Or was Ladeeda only for politics and republics? He is tired, he cannot remember, the billowing movement of the treetops is lulling him asleep. But again to please Minnie he makes a heroic effort to keep awake and to listen to her and to go on reading the papers. He is after all a hero. Also: he feels she is hiding something. If he lets her talk she may betray herself.

—It says here, Mr. Binchey, that the I.R.A. blew up a young private soldier of the Ulster Defence Regiment as he was making a regular call on a sixty-eight-year-old house-bound widow. He was off duty and on a tractor and going to chop wood, a daily task to help the aged widow. All U.D.R. men have been warned (Mr. Binchey has had to help her with some of the words) to exercise caution in carrying out spare-time errands of mercy to help the aged and infirm.

—It's in an English newspaper, Minnie.

—Still.

The gullies of her cheeks are again wet but not, this time, with laughter.

—For all those blackguards care, Mr. Binchey, all of us old people could starve or freeze in our houses. If we had a house left to starve in. She has betrayed herself. He is wide awake. The tree-tops are still, or seem to be. The town below is still unviolated. The gun attack which killed three men in the Belfast pub owned by former Stormont minister, Roy Bradford, is believed to have been the work of a Republican group seeking vengeance for the bombing of the White Fort Inn in Andersonstown in which two men died and six were seriously injured. Come landlord fill the flowing bowl, and an Irishman's pub is no longer his castle: it was all so unexpected, in seconds men who had been enjoying themselves and watching athletics on the teevee were slumped dead or wounded at the counter.

—What was that you said, Minnie?

He is still reading the paper.

—Sacred Heart of Jesus, they'll murder me, Mr. Binchey. You weren't supposed to know until you were up and about.

—Know what, Minnie?

—They burned the house, Mr. Binchey.

—They burned the house.

—Since then we've been living in Judge Flynn's.

—In Judge Flynn's.

All except Mr. Binchey, Mr. Binchey. He's living in the barn to get the repairs going.

—Repairs. Judge Flynn is a good man.

—He is, Mr. Binchey. And his wife's a lovely woman, too.

—She is.

—It was the fellow with the gasmask. And the shotgun. He said they should burn the house to destroy fingerprints. And the Corkman laughed and said he thought that was the funniest thing he ever heard.

—Fingerprints.

—Mr. Binchey tried to get at them. It was then they shot him in the left knee.

—But Minnie, they can't destroy footprints.

—No, Mr. Binchey.

She doesn't know what he's talking about.

Convert the Orangemen, Mr. Binchey. Declare a Republic, Mr. Binchey. Burn the house, Mr. Binchey, to destroy fingerprints.

—They burned Portrush too, Mr. Binchey.

—They did indeed, Minnie. So why should we worry. I read in the papers about Portrush.

Eight buildings in the centre of Portrush, County Antrim, one of the major holiday resorts in Northern Ireland, were destroyed after a telephone warning that ten bombs had been placed in the town by the Provisional I.R.A.

You may talk of Bundoran, of Warrenpoint and Bangor, but come to Portrush if you want to be gay. Yes, Billy me boy, put your hand in your pocket, just spend a few ha'pence and come to the say.

That was in a comic song about the seaside resorts of Ulster.

Bracing breezes, silvery sands, booming breakers, lovely lands, come to . . .

No, that was about Bundoran where the Catholics go, not Portrush where the Protestants go.

But the Orangemen could now, couldn't they, burn Bundoran? Or pubs in Dublin? Or the Ark of the Covenant if they could find it, or the Pearly Gates or Uncle Tom's Cabin or the tumble-down shack in Athlone or the house that Jack built or the little old mud cabin on the hill? What anyway do people want with pubs, or all those houses, or hotels or churches or schools or libraries or happy holidays? Burn the bloody lot. Wipe out all the world's fingerprints.

The papers slither on to the floor and he falls half-asleep and Minnie sits there and cries silently.

There is a place in the lake called the Blue Stones. Twenty feet out from the shore and in shallow water two conical blue rocks stand up a few feet above the surface and look at each other as if they were in love, lovers turned to stone and unable for all eternity to touch or taste.

When he was twelve years old he owned a Brownie camera, a birthday present. His pal, Tony, and himself, both trouserless, waded out to the Blue Stones. Tony balanced on one, he on the other. He peered and clicked and snapped Tony balancing, bare-legged, shirt-tail fluttering, and the snapshot was no sooner taken than Tony fell off into the water. Sitting on the shore in the July sunshine, Tony naked, his clothes spread out on a bush, they laughed and dried themselves and ate toffee and drank lemonade.

He can't now in his half-sleep remember when exactly it was that he had the terrible dream about Tony.

He, not Tony, is, in the dream, sitting alone by the great glowing range where his father used to stir the porridge. He is reading a book. Out in a scullery a voice keeps chanting, like

the voice of a schoolboy learning something by rote. He listens
more carefully. It is Tony's voice. He tiptoes to the door of the
scullery. Tony is standing by a blackboard with chalk markings
on it. He has in his hand a long, yellow, wooden pointer. He is
spelling out something but it makes no sense. Then, as he
watches, black hair grows on Tony's face and his upper teeth
protrude like fangs: and he awakes screaming that Tony's going
mad, Tony's going mad.

The odd thing is that at the age of eighteen Tony did go mad.
A premonition? Or was the dream before or after the event?
Either way, that was the end of the laughter of the water and the
Blue Stones. A dream, like the dream of the white house.
Somewhere, somewhere he still has that snapshot.

His eyes open again. Minnie has dried her tears. When I was
a teacher, pin-stripe and pince-nez, my jokes in class were well-
known, even became proverbial, so I may have given something
to my town to be remembered as long as the last of my students
live, then to be forgotten or attributed to someone else. Cathy
comes in and runs to Minnie. At least my body will go intact
to lie beside her, membrane by member, ghosts, to the final,
far beyond this partial, day of doom. Gary comes in and runs
to his grandfather's bedside. But by the living Jesus they should
not have touched my house, my living dream seen across
water and through tall reeds and beech trees, they should not,
they should not have touched my living dream, mad Minahan,
Bertie Bigfeet, Creepy Corkman whoever you are, I will see
you all in hell. Her son comes in hobbling on a half-crutch.
Followed by his wife, as rich a red wine as ever, carrying parcels
and grandfather's clothes.

—Minnie, Minnie Brown, Cathy sings, we're home again
from Dungloe town.

The crabs are dead within the last hour. The oxalis is past its best. The house is burned. There is no laughter around the Blue Stones. The lake will never be the same again. Tony the madman roars through his dreams. Oh, the sights that we see as we wait here for death on the treacherous waves.

—But not destroyed, his son says.

More than my town, more than my family, my dream of a white house.

—They did their worst, his son says. But they should have brought a professional pyromaniac with them. We kept it out of the papers.

—You could have told me.

By the living Jesus they should not have tampered with my dream.

—You had enough to recover from. We thought it better.

Minnie and his daughter-in-law and the children are by the window laughing at the antics of a crew of magpies in the swaying treetops. The town, still undisturbed, is far below. His son gathers the newspapers from the carpet, stooping and rising again with some difficulty. He says: You knew them.

—Two of them. That'll do to begin with.

—I felt you might know them.

—Oh, I've been watching people in this town for a long time. Their faces. Their families. The books they read. Even their feet. If you looked at little else but the way people walk you could write a history of a place. Boots, boots, boots marching up and down again. Kipling, you know.

Patiently his son says: I know.

And through a gap in the reeds he looks, as he waits for the perch, across the water at the white house. Reeds make one frame for the picture. Beech trees, set back from the avenue that leads up to the house, make another. He envies the people who own it, the lawn and flower-beds before it, the barns and varied outbuildings behind it. He has missed a strike. Tony is laughing. And the most beautiful thing of all, cutting across a corner of the lawn, a small brook tumbling down to join the lake. To have your own stream on your own lawn is the height of everything.

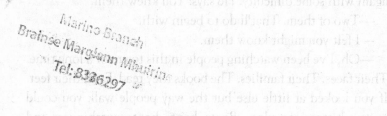

Turnpike Books has been established to publish new editions of classic Northern Irish novels and short stories.

Also available

THE LOUGHSIDERS

Shan Bullock

"One of the best novels that rural Ireland has provoked."
Benedict Kiely, 'Irish Times'

Few writers have captured the comedy of country life, or the frustrations and daily struggles of small farmers, as faithfully as Shan Bullock. In *The Loughsiders* Bullock drew on the speech, as much as the landscape, of the area around Lough Erne in his most complete novel with its understanding of the Ulster character and ironic observation of Ulster life.

"Deserves a significant place in the history of Ulster fiction"
Culture Northern Ireland

Richard Jebb has returned from the United States to the quiet beauty, unchanging rhythms of life and close horizons of a small farming community along the shore of Lough Erne. Richard silently harbours larger ambitions and after his proposal to Rachel Nixon, the daughter of a neighbouring farmer, is refused he seizes his opportunity when her father dies without leaving a will. Complex and scheming, Richard manipulates the destinies of the Nixon family and his patient intrigue changes the lives of all those who live by the lough.

Shan Bullock was born in Fermanagh in 1865, the son of a farmer who became steward of the Crom estate. He spent most of his life in London working for the civil service and also wrote literary journalism.

Bullock was awarded a MBE for his part in the Irish Home Rule Convention of 1917 and 1918, and was made a member of the Irish Academy of Letters in 1933. Shan Bullock died in 1935.

Also available

THE WAYWARD MAN

St John Ervine

"The only Belfast writer who has tried at all to bottle the 'realism' of the city."

Sean O'Faolain

Robert Dunwoody has inherited his father's love of the sea and restless spirit while his mother dreams that he will play a part in their family business. Robert rebels against the world of small shopkeepers to follow the harsh, dangerous live of a sailor. After years away, travelling across the oceans and as a hobo in the United States, Robert returns to Belfast and is trapped into marriage and a shop of his own. Can he free himself to return to the world beyond Belfast's streets and return to the joys of an independent life?

"He never fails as the interpreter of the grimness and the nobility, the shrewdness and the simplicity, of the dwellers in Belfast."

'Times Literary Supplement'

St John Ervine was the forerunner of Northern Ireland's distinctive literature and the first writer to capture the voices and character of Belfast. St John Ervine was born in 1883 in east Belfast. On moving to London as a teenager he met George Bernard Shaw and joined the Fabian Society. Ervine's first play, 'Mixed Marriage', was produced by Dublin's Abbey Theatre in 1911 pioneering realism on the Irish stage.

Ervine was a prolific writer of journalism and novels, as well as biographies of Parnell, Lord Craigavon and George Bernard Shaw. By the 1940s Ervine was Northern Ireland's most prominent writer. He died in 1971.